Jaden

Jaden

ROTTEN SCHOOL

series:

#1. The Big Blueberry Barf-Off!

#2. The Great Smelling Bee

#3. The Good, the Bad and the Very Slimy

#4. Lose, Team, Lose!

#5. Shake, Rattle, & Hurl!

#6. The Heinie Prize

#7. Dudes, The School Is Haunted!

#8. The Teacher from Heck

#9. Party Poopers

#10. The Rottenest Angel

#11. Punk'd and Skunked

#12. Battle of the Dum Diddys

#13. Got Cake?

Jaden

ROTTEN SCHOOL

GROWTH · LEARNING · PIZZA!

NIGHT OF THE CREEPY THINGS

R.L. STINE

Illustrations by Trip Park

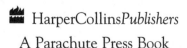

HarperCollins*Publishers*

A Parachute Press Book

For Hampton
–TP

Library of Congress Cataloging-in-Publication Data is available.
ISBN 978-0-06-123272-5 (trade bdg.) — ISBN 978-0-06-123273-2 (lib. bdg.)

Cover and interior design by mjcdesign
1 2 3 4 5 6 7 8 9 10

First Edition

GROWTH · LEARNING · PIZZA!

—: CONTENTS :—

Morning Announcements 1

1. The Mummy's Revenge 3

2. The Beast from Preschool 8

3. Help! It's Stuck to My Foot! 14

4. Revenge of the Warts 20

5. Attack of the Toadstool People 24

6. Attack of the Apples Falling
   on Your Head 30

7. Beauty and the Beast II 35

8. Don't Tell Anyone 41

9. Giant Monster Ants Up Close 47

10. Me, the Werewolf 52

11. Morning of the Robot Worm 54

12. Lousy Night at the Zoo 62

13. Attack of the Root Beer 65

14. The Making of *Horror Zoo* 70

15. Scream, Sherman, Scream! 72

16. Snakes on My Leg 79

17. Movie in My Head 82

18. Escape of the Mad, Mad,
    Mad Gorilla 87

19. Attack of the Klutz! 93

20. Scream, Feenman and Crench,
    Scream! 97

21. I'm Scared! 102

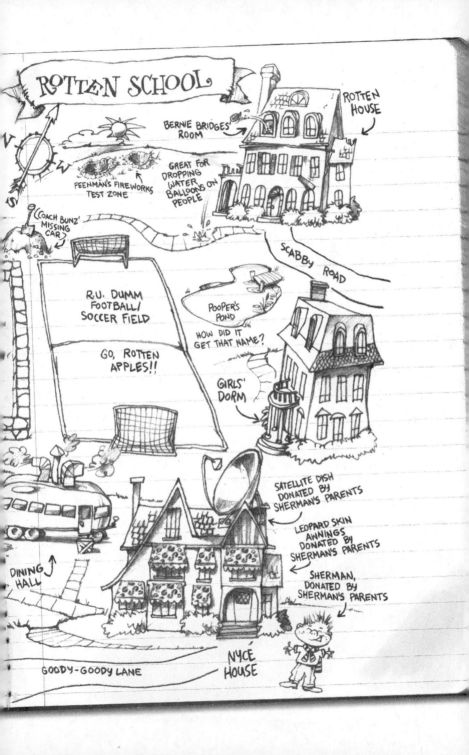

MORNING ANNOUNCEMENTS

Good morning, Rotten Students. This is your beloved Headmaster Upchuck. Please—no standing ovation this morning. I know how much you admire me. I wish I liked kids. It would make my job so much easier.

But anyway, please listen to this morning's Morning Announcements...

Will the students who buried Coach Manley Bunz's car under the soccer field please return the shovels? Chef Baloney needs them to dish out today's lunch.

1

Nurse Hanley would like to remind all fourth graders that you are not supposed to be giving each other measles shots. That is *her* job.

Just because the fourth grader known as Beast ate a cockroach at dinner last night doesn't mean that *everyone* has to do it. There aren't enough cockroaches to go around.

$ $ $ Assistant Headmaster Skruloose has learned that all the money donated to the Bernie Bridges Save-A-Life Foundation is being kept by Bernie Bridges. Please do not give any more money to this charity.

The Sixth Grade Long-Distance Burping Competition will be held today after lunch. Please remember that contestants must stand at least six inches apart from one another.

Finally, Parents Visiting Day has been canceled for next week because your parents *begged* us not to force them to see you.

Chapter 1

THE MUMMY'S REVENGE

Well, dudes, as our scary story starts, big Joe Sweety was sound asleep in his desk chair. Sweety falls asleep every night the minute he starts to do his homework.

And there he was, snoring a little, his mouth open, eyes shut, dirty brown hair falling over his face. And there we were—my buddies Feenman, Crench, and me—sneaking silently into his dorm room to turn him into a mummy.

Yes, a mummy.

Don't worry. I'll explain.

As you may know, you *never* call Joe Sweety *Sweety*.

That's because Joe is the biggest, toughest, meanest dude at Rotten School. He's so tough, he can slap you with his *tongue*—and it really hurts.

If he steps on your foot, it isn't a foot anymore. It's a pancake with bones.

Joe is so tough, his mother calls him *sir*!

The best time to hang out with Sweety is when he's asleep. That's why my buddies and I waited until we saw his head droop. Then we crawled in through his window.

I had a plan that couldn't fail. I *always* have plans that can't fail.

You've probably heard of me. Bernie Bridges. I may be the brainiest, coolest, most *awesome* kid at Rotten School—but I never brag.

Tonight we were starting to make the best horror video ever made by fourth graders. That's why we needed to turn the Big Sweety into a mummy.

So we climbed into his room, and I handed a roll of bandages to Crench. "Let's get started," I whispered.

I turned and saw Feenman blowing his nose on the drapes. "Why are you doing that?" I asked.

"Cuz I have a cold," Feenman replied.

Feenman is an awesome dude. But I've seen him blow his nose on the drapes even when he *didn't* have a cold!

He wiped his nose on the back of his hand.

"Wrap Sweety up," I told Crench. "Make it look good."

I was the writer, the producer, and the director of this video. I knew it would be great even before we started. Sweety was gonna be the scariest mummy in movie history!

Why were we making this scary video?

Why were kids all over campus out terrifying one another every night?

Don't worry. I'll explain later.

Crench carefully lifted one of Sweety's big arms and started to wrap it. Sweety let out a snort, but his eyes didn't open. Crench began to wrap white bandages around the big dude's chest.

"Lookin' good," I whispered.

Sweety snored away as Crench wrapped his other arm and started tying the bandages around his head. Sweety looked more like an ancient mummy every second.

Scary. Totally scary.

But then I heard Feenman make a noise behind me. It sounded like *Ah–Ah-Ah.*

I turned—and Feenman made a much *louder* noise....

AH~AH~AHHHH~ CHOOOOOOOOOOOOOEY!

Feenman's sneeze rattled the windows, knocked over a lamp, and sprayed the front of my T-shirt with about a gallon of snot.

And it woke up Joe Sweety.

The Big Sweety let out a growl, tore at his bandages, jumped to his feet—and grabbed me by the throat. "*Revenge of the Mummy!*" he screamed.

Gasping for air, I turned to Feenman. "Are you getting this?" I choked out. "This is perfect! Are you getting this on video?"

Sweety started to rattle me like a saltshaker. I saw Feenman's mouth drop open.

"Uh-oh," he muttered. "Sorry, Bernie. I forgot the camcorder."

Chapter 2

THE BEAST FROM PRESCHOOL

Yes, life can be scary these days at Rotten School.

Why were kids terrifying one another every night? Well, I promised I'd explain.

It all started on Welcome Back Day.

That's a tradition started many years ago by our school's founder, Mr. I. B. Rotten. Every year Headmaster Upchuck welcomes back some dude or dudette who graduated from our school.

The person gives a speech to the whole school. You know. To inspire us. To tell us how being in Rotten School prepares us to go out into the world and do great things someday.

I remember the speaker from Welcome Back Day last year. It was a woman who had a knitting needle stuck in her nose. She talked about how you can still have an awesome life, even with a knitting needle in your nose.

Two years ago the speaker was the guy who invented diapers for horses.

We have a *lot* of cool graduates from our school.

But *this* year's visitor was the coolest of all, even cooler than the horse-diaper guy. And we were totally crazed and excited because…

…this year's speaker was our favorite horror movie director, Mr. B. A. Gool.

As we all piled into the auditorium, my buddies and I argued over which was Gool's creepiest film.

"It's gotta be *The Beast from Preschool!*" Crench said. "Remember that dude? He was only four years old, but he could bite your throat out."

My buddy Belzer gave Crench a shove. "That wasn't scary at all," he said. "Know which one totally freaked me out? *I'll Eat Your Face for Breakfast.* After that movie, I couldn't eat breakfast for a *month!*"

"Too babyish," Crench said. "My two-year-old sister liked that one. Gool's scariest film has to be *My HAIR Is ALIVE!* I couldn't sleep for six weeks. I knew if I went to sleep, my hair would strangle me."

They turned to me. "What do you think, Big B?" Belzer asked.

Before I could answer, Sherman Oaks bumped up between us. He tossed back his blond hair and flashed us his perfect, sixty-five-tooth smile.

"Anyone got change for a hundred?" he asked. He waved a hundred-dollar bill in my face. "Or can anyone change this *five*-hundred-dollar bill?" He waved it under my nose.

Sherman does that every day. He doesn't want change. He just likes to make me drool.

He is the richest kid at Rotten School. He's so rich, he pays a kid to burp for him.

"Dudes, check this out," he said. He stuck out his left sneaker.

I saw a small silver screen on top of the sneaker. "What's that for?" I asked. "A viewer so you can see what you're stepping into?"

"The sneaker is a DVD player," Sherman said. "I

downloaded twenty-eight B. A. Gool movies onto it. I watch them on my shoe while I walk to class."

Sherman raised the shoe higher. "See? The volume control is on the toe part," he said. "The shoe cost five thousand dollars. My parents sent it to me cuz they think they can buy my love."

"Cool," I said. "What does the other sneaker do?"

"It's an MP3 player," Sherman said. "I downloaded two thousand songs onto it."

We jammed into the auditorium and found seats near the front. Headmaster Upchuck was already on the stage. He's only about three feet tall. He's so short, he has to stand on a ladder to look in the mirror to comb his hair!

The Headmaster stood on a tall stool, trying to reach the microphone.

I could tell Belzer was excited. He kept kicking the seat in front of him. "What do you think B. A. Gool looks like?" he asked. "He's *got* to be way weird, right?"

"He probably wears a long, black cape," Crench said.

"Maybe he has fangs," Feenman said. "And really

pale white skin . . . because he has no blood. And they'll have to keep the auditorium lights off because bright light will melt him."

"I'll bet he's like some kinda monster," Belzer said. "He's got to be way weird to make movies like those."

Up on the stage, Headmaster Upchuck tapped the microphone. "Welcome back to Welcome Back Day," he said. "I want to welcome back everyone to our Welcome Back celebration."

His stool tilted. He started to fall off.

Everyone cheered.

But he caught himself by grabbing on to the microphone.

Everyone groaned.

"And now," he said, "let's welcome back to Welcome Back Day one of our most famous graduates. Let's give a real Rotten welcome to . . . B. A. Gool!"

We all cheered and jumped up and down and went nuts.

And there he came, B. A. Gool, walking onto the stage . . . and everyone *gasped* in *shock*!

Chapter 3

HELP! IT'S STUCK TO MY FOOT!

Everyone gasped in shock . . . because he looked *totally normal!*

He wasn't weird in any way. He was tall and thin. He had wavy brown hair, wore black-rimmed glasses, and had a nice smile as he stepped up to the microphone.

No black cape. No fangs. He wore a pale blue shirt under a gray sports jacket and faded jeans.

"My name is B. A. Gool," he said in a soft voice. "And my job is to scare you!"

A few kids laughed. But most of us just stared at

him. He wasn't scary at all!

"Kids ask me all the time where I get my ideas for my scary movies," he continued. "Well, a lot of my *scariest* ideas came from right here at Rotten School."

"YEAAAA!" Belzer cheered and kicked the seat in front of him.

I glanced down the row. At the end, my friend Chipmunk had his hands covering his face. He scrunched down low, hiding behind the seat backs.

Chipmunk is the shyest kid at Rotten School. He's so shy, he has trouble talking to *himself*! Poor guy. I could see that he was really scared of B. A. Gool.

"I lived in Rotten House," B. A. Gool said, "and my room was very crowded—with *insects*! At night I would wake up with bugs and worms crawling all over my body . . . in my hair . . . in my ears . . . and on my tongue."

"Me too!" someone shouted.

In the next row, my friend Beast shouted, "Did you *eat* any of them?"

A lot of kids laughed. But we knew Beast wasn't

joking. Beast is a little strange. We're not sure if he's human or not. He's way too hairy to be a human. And he chews the bark off trees.

"Mr. Gool!" Beast shouted. "What did you do with the bugs you pulled from your nose?"

Gool squinted at Beast. "Good question. I'll answer your questions later," he said. "Anyway, that's where I got the ideas for my first two movies—*Bugs on My Face* and *Bugs on My Face II: Night of the Living Bugs*."

The whole auditorium went nuts, cheering and clapping. My buddies and I have watched those movies at least ten times—and then we itch for a week!

"This is a *wonderful* school for horror," Gool said. "I remember one night in fifth grade. I went for a late-night swim in Pooper's Pond. I dove in. And when I came up, some kind of slimy, sticky jellyfish creature had attached itself to the bottom of my foot.

"Man, did that *sting*! I sat down and tried to pull it off. But it stuck to my foot. My friends tried to tug it off. The slimy thing wouldn't budge. It was stuck tight."

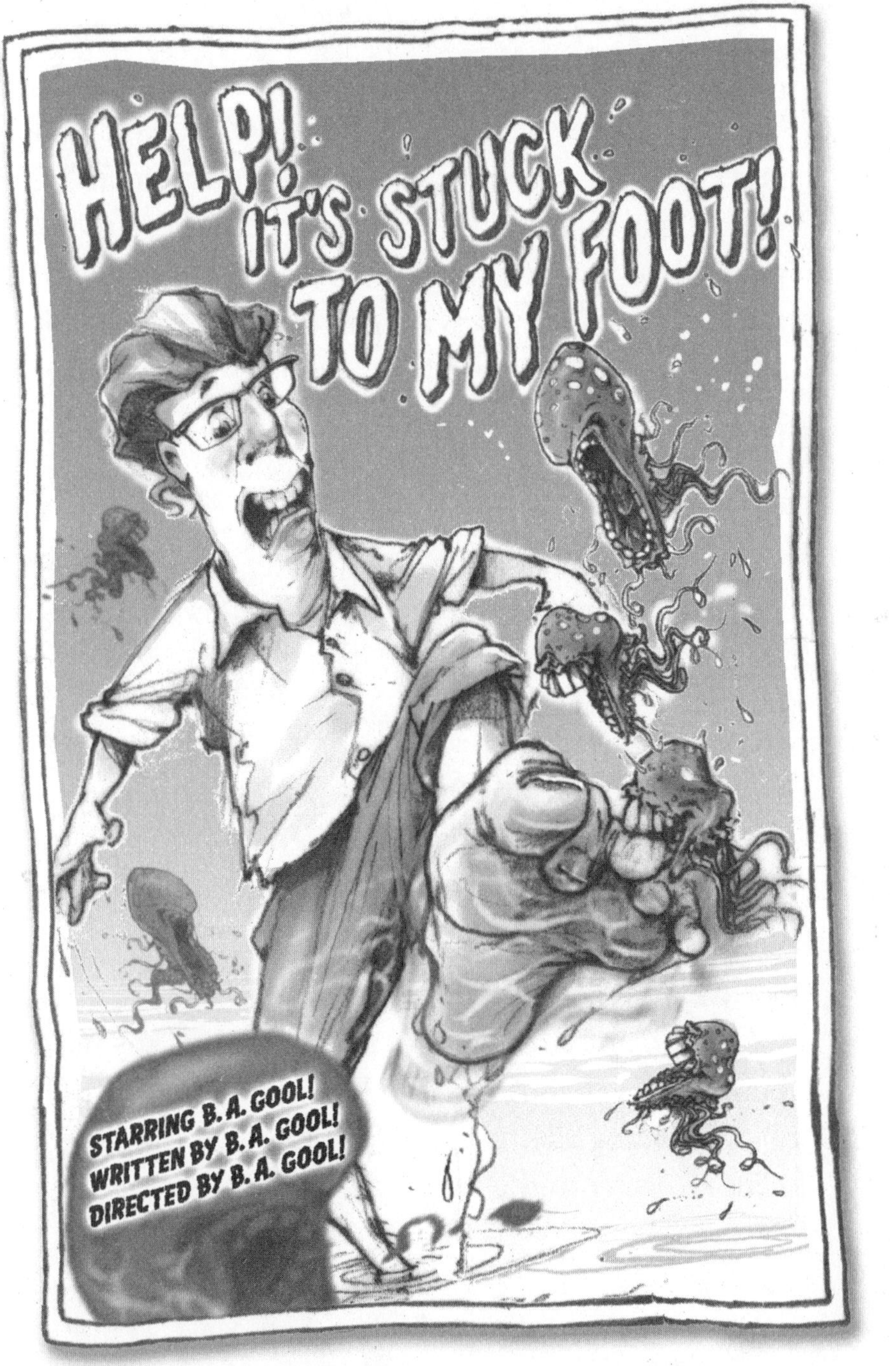
HELP! IT'S STUCK TO MY FOOT!
STARRING B. A. GOOL!
WRITTEN BY B. A. GOOL!
DIRECTED BY B. A. GOOL!

"Finally they helped carry me to the nurse," Gool said. "She tried to cut it off—but it wouldn't *cut!*"

He held up his left shoe. "I'm still *wearing* it!" he cried. "I've had this creature stuck on the bottom of my foot for *twenty years!* That's why I have to wear such big shoes."

Everyone oohed and aahed.

"But it gave me the idea for my biggest film," Gool said. "I'm sure you all remember *HELP! It's STUCK to My FOOT!*"

Again the auditorium went nuts. Everyone stood up and cheered and shouted.

Everyone except Chipmunk.

Now he was hiding *under* his seat with his head buried in his hands.

"So, enjoy the horror, everyone!" Gool shouted. "You've come to the right school!"

We all settled back down into our seats. I saw Beast pull a fat, brown bug from his hair and toss it onstage. It landed on B. A. Gool's neck. I don't think he saw it.

"And now I have big news..." he said. "I have a big announcement for all you Rotten Students."

An announcement?

A hush fell over the auditorium.

We had no idea that B. A. Gool was about to change our lives.

Chapter 4

REVENGE OF THE WARTS

"I think it's time you proved just what a scary place this is!" Gool said. "So I'm inviting all you Rotten Students to make your own horror videos."

We just stared at him. Was he *serious*?

"Make the scariest videos you can," Gool continued. "On Halloween night I'll come back to Rotten School. And I will judge them."

"What do we win?" Joe Sweety shouted.

"Could I have that bug back?" Beast asked, pointing to the bug on Gool's neck.

Gool sipped from a bottle of water. "The boy or

girl who makes the best horror video," he said, "will win a small role in my next movie. As you probably know, the movie is called *EEK IV: Revenge of the Warts.*"

Everyone cheered and clapped.

Sherman Oaks leaned forward from the row behind me. "I've been watching *EEK III: The Warts Are ALIVE!* on my shoe," he said. "It's way scary. Made my whole foot shake!"

But I wasn't interested in Sherman's shoe. I was thinking hard about the video contest. I knew I could win it. And once I had a small part in B. A. Gool's movie, I knew I could talk him into giving me a *bigger* part.

Bernie B. was going to be a movie star!

Kids stood up and started back to class. I pushed my way up to the stage. I put on my best smile—the one with the adorable dimples in both cheeks—and stepped up to B. A. Gool.

"Nice to meet you," I said, sticking out my hand for a handshake. "I'm Bernie Bridges. You can call me Bernie. I'm your contest winner. I just want to say thank you in advance. I'd like to tell you a few of

my best movie ideas. And I ..."

But he wasn't listening to me.

He was gazing at Beast with a big smile on his face. Beast stepped onto the stage, and Gool patted him on one hairy shoulder. "Nice costume," B. A. Gool said. "I like all the bristly animal hair and those insane monster teeth! Great costume, kid. You totally scared me."

He hurried away.

I burst out laughing. Of course, Beast wasn't *wearing* a costume! Actually, he was looking a lot better than usual.

"Beast, I think he liked you," I said.

Beast licked my hand. "Thanks, Bernie." He pulled another bug out of his hair and offered it to me.

"No thanks," I said. "I'm a vegetarian."

I grinned at him. And suddenly . . . suddenly I had a fabulous idea for a horror movie.

Chapter 5

ATTACK OF THE TOADSTOOL PEOPLE

You probably go home every day after school. Our school is a boarding school. That means we all *live* here.

It's totally sweet. No parents. Just one grown-up—Mrs. Heinie, our dorm mother, snoops and spies on us and tells us what we shouldn't be doing that we do anyway.

My buddies and I live in Rotten House. Just like B. A. Gool did when he went to school here. That night, I called my friends into my room to tell them my movie idea.

24

Feenman and Crench sat on the floor and leaned back against a wall. They were sitting under my favorite poster—the big poster of ME! They kept punching each other in the shoulder to see who would scream first. It's kind of a sport.

Chipmunk sat in my armchair. Beast dropped down onto the edge of the bed and started pulling feathers out of my pillow. Billy the Brain stood by the door, reading a book.

"What's that book about?" I asked Billy.

He shrugged. "Beats me. It's in French."

See? I told you he's a total brainiac.

I passed out cans of Foamy Root Beer. It's our fave. The foam is so thick, it stays on your face for hours.

"Where's Belzer?" Feenman asked, landing a hard punch on Crench's shoulder.

Crench had tears rolling down his face, but he didn't scream.

At that moment, Belzer stumbled into the room. He carried a huge metal bucket. He dropped it in front of Beast.

"I picked as many as I could find," he said.

"Good work, Belzer," I said. I touched knuckles with him.

Belzer was sweating and panting hard. Guess the bucket was heavy.

"What's in there?" Feenman asked. He leaned forward and stuck his face into the bucket. "Ohhh, yuck! That's totally *sick!*"

"No way it's sick," I said. I reached in. "Haven't you ever seen a toadstool before?" I held up a mushroom.

"Gross," Chipmunk said, hiding his eyes.

"The toadstool is actually a member of the marsupial family," Billy the Brain said. "It's related to the Australian kangaroo. Its brain is located under the floppy cap, which protects it."

"Wow. Billy knows *everything!*" Crench said.

"Billy, I thought a toadstool was a mushroom," I said.

Belzer shook his head and moaned. "All I know is, the stupid things squirted toadstool juice all over my school blazer."

Poor guy had brown stains up and down his jacket.

"It's worth it, Belzer," I said, slapping him on the

back. "This is gonna help us win the Horror Movie Contest."

"I don't get it," Crench said. "You're gonna make a movie about a bucket of disgusting toadstools?"

"Better than that," I said. "Listen up, dudes. Listen to pure genius. Our video is going to be called *Attack of the Toadstool People*."

They stared at me. Feenman and Crench stopped punching each other's shoulders.

"We're gonna paint faces on all the toadstools and shoot them up close," I said. "The toadstool people will attack the school—and Beast will be their leader."

Feenman frowned. "Beast? Why Beast? Don't you want a *human* star?"

"Are you kidding?" I said. "We can't *lose* with Beast as the star. He *already* scared B. A. Gool!"

Chipmunk hugged himself. I could see he was shivering. "Too scary for me," he said. He dove under the bed.

"Chipper—come out of there!" I cried. I tried to pull him out by the feet.

"Let go, Bernie. I'm not coming out till the

movie is finished!" he called in a soft, trembling voice.

"Hel-lo?...Bernie? I think the movie *is* finished," Feenman said.

I spun around. "Huh? What do you mean?"

Feenman pointed at the bucket. Empty.

Beast had a big grin on his face. "All gone," he said.

Beast ate the entire bucket of toadstools.

He wiped his mouth with the back of one hand. "I like 'em better with sauce!" he said.

Chapter 6

ATTACK OF THE APPLES FALLING ON YOUR HEAD

I took a walk on the Great Lawn. Walking always helps me think. I needed a new movie idea—something Beast wouldn't eat.

It was a clear, cool October night. Stars twinkled in a cold, black sky. The apple trees along the path shivered in the breeze. Every once in a while I heard the *thud* of an apple hitting the ground.

Attack of the Apples Falling on Your Head?

No. Not scary enough.

I had my head down, eyes on the grass, thinking hard. And I bumped right into Jennifer Ecch.

"Raise your head. Look into the camera," she said.

"Excuse me?"

She had a camcorder pressed to her face. She had it pointed at me. I tried to duck away, but she followed me with the lens.

"Sugar Nose, aren't you *thrilled* that I'm making a movie about you?" Jennifer asked.

"Don't call me Sugar Nose," I groaned.

Jennifer is the biggest, hulkiest, strongest girl in school. For exercise, she pulls *trees* out of the ground! And that's just for a warm-up!

I call her Nightmare Girl because she's totally in love with me. Do you know how embarrassing it is to be in fourth grade and have a girl call you Sugar Nose in front of all your friends?

I covered my face with one arm. "Jennifer, please stop!" I cried.

"I can't stop, Honey Breath," she said. "I'm taping your every move. You're the star of my horror video."

"No, I'm not," I said. "I don't want to be in your movie. I'm making my own movie. Please—go away."

She got a pouty look on her face. "Cutie Patootie, don't you even want to know what my video is called?"

"No, I don't," I said. "And don't call me Cutie Patootie."

"It's called *Bite Night*," she said.

I stared at her. "Hey, not bad," I said. "Good title. Is it a vampire film?"

She grabbed me by the shoulders and pulled me into a tall hedge. "Here, Sugar Nose. I'll show you what *Bite Night* is about."

BITE! BITE! BITE! BITE!

"OWWWW!"

I howled. "STOP! I'm begging you—STOP!"

I squirmed and struggled, but I couldn't get away. She wouldn't stop biting my neck. She had huge horse teeth, and I think she sharpened them with a file!

"OW! STOP! STOP!"

I cried. You're giving me RABIES!"

Finally she pulled her teeth back. She made some loud, lip-smacking noises. Then she checked her camcorder.

"Good scene," she said. "You did some good screaming. But I think we need to shoot it a few more times—just to make sure."

Chapter 7

BEAUTY AND THE BEAST II

The next morning, I woke up with bruises on my neck and an awesome idea for a horror video.

Belzer brought me breakfast in bed, and I hummed all through my scrambled eggs, bacon, sausages, potatoes, sun-dried tomatoes, cheese Danish, blueberry muffins, cornflakes, waffles, and toast.

Just a light breakfast for me today. I was too excited about my idea to eat very much.

I pulled on my school uniform, tightened the tie around my neck—the beautiful mix of purple, green, and yellow, the school colors—and hurried outside to find April-May June.

April-May June is the coolest, hottest girl at Rotten School. She's wicked nuts about me. Only she doesn't know it yet.

I saw her across the Great Lawn, hurrying to class. Her blond ponytail swayed behind her. Her blue eyes sparkled like...like...blue eyes.

"April-May—wait up!" I shouted.

She started to run faster. She always plays hard-to-get. It's proof that she's crazy about me.

I caught up with her and flashed her my best smile. "Nice morning, isn't it?"

"It was a perfect morning till this second," she said.

She has an awesome sense of humor.

April-May's eyes narrowed at me. She made a disgusted face. "Bernie, what are all those bandages on your neck?"

"Oh...uh...I had a biting accident," I said.

Her mouth dropped open. Her chewing gum fell out. "You were biting yourself? I *knew* you had a big mouth—but that's *ridiculous*!" She tossed back her head and roared with laughter.

I told you she has a great sense of humor.

I could feel myself blushing. "Actually, it's just mosquito bites," I lied. "I've got to get some bug spray. I'm so sweet, mosquitoes can't resist me!"

She picked her chewing gum off the walk and popped it back into her mouth. "Bernie, what do you want?" she asked.

"I know you're *dying* to star in my horror movie," I said. "But you're too shy to ask me. Right?"

She pulled the gum from her mouth and stuck it onto my forehead.

"Is that a yes or a no?" I asked.

"I'd rather eat my toenails whole," she said.

"Aha! I *knew* you'd be interested!" I cried. "You'll love this idea. It's *Beauty and the Beast II*, starring you and Beast. Perfect, right? You'll play Beauty."

"No way," she said.

"Don't worry," I told her. "We'll clean Beast up so he won't be as scary as in real life."

"No way," she said. "I won't do a movie with the kid who ate the class hamster."

"It was an accident," I told her. "Beast just wanted a *taste*!"

"No way, Bernie," April-May said, shaking her head. "I promised Sherman Oaks I'd star in *his* video. Sherman is gonna win, and he said he'll let me be in B. A. Gool's new movie."

I rolled my eyes. "What kind of horror movie is Sherman making? His life story?"

"Ha-ha, Bernie," April-May sneered. "You're about as funny as gas pains."

See? She's totally nuts about me. She just doesn't know how to show it.

April-May pulled the gum off my forehead, popped it back into her beautiful mouth, and hurried away.

I took two steps toward the School House—and two strong hands pulled me into the hedge. I let out a gasp. "Jennifer!"

The Ecch had me by the neck.

"Honey Eyebrows, did I hear you correctly?" she asked. "Were you telling April-May that you want ME to star in *Beauty and the Beast II*?"

"Yes, we're gonna call it *Beast and the Beast*!" I joked.

Uh-oh.

Bad joke.

Very bad joke.

"Jennifer—please—" I begged. "You can take a joke—right?"

"Sure, I can," she said. "But right now, let's rehearse another scene from MY movie!"

Chapter 8

DON'T TELL ANYONE

That afternoon, I spotted Sherman Oaks's pal Wes Updood. He was setting up equipment behind the Student Center. I jogged over to him.

"Whussup, dude?" I said to Wes Updood.

He nodded at me. "Hearty granola," he said. "Bucket of slops. Ya know?"

"For sure," I replied.

Wes is the coolest, hippest guy at Rotten School. He is so totally cool, no one understands what he's saying!

"What is this stuff?" I asked, pointing at the tall

lamps and boxes of electronics in front of him.

"Shake your salt," Wes said. "Shake your salt and pepper. But don't shake your booty."

"No problem," I said.

"Shaker Heights," Wes said. "Be there or be square. Know what I mean?"

"Akron, Ohio," I replied. I was trying to get on his wavelength.

He burst out laughing. "Akron, Ohio?" he repeated. "Ha-ha-ha-ha. Good one! Lake Erie, dude!" He laughed some more.

Luckily, Sherman Oaks came strolling up to us. He slapped my shoulder. "Bernie, old buddy," he said. "You came to try out for my movie? You're a little early. Auditions don't start till three."

I blinked. "Try out for your movie?"

"I guess you just can't wait to be in it," Sherman said.

"Mahwah, New Jersey," Wes Updood muttered. He pulled more equipment from a large trunk.

"You're joking," I told Sherman. "Why would anyone want to be in *your* movie when they can be in *mine*?"

Sherman snickered in reply. "What's your movie called, Bernie?"

"I'm not telling," I said. "What's *your* movie called?"

"*Don't Tell Anyone*," Sherman replied.

"I won't tell anyone," I said. "What's it called?"

"*Don't Tell Anyone*," Sherman said again.

I raised my right hand in the air. "I promise I won't tell. What's your movie called?"

"*Don't Tell Anyone*," Sherman repeated.

"Okay, forget it," I muttered. "*Don't* tell me what it's called. I don't care. What makes you think you can do a movie that's as good as mine?"

He snickered again. "Maybe because of this little contraption my parents bought for me," he said.

I stared at the equipment Wes was setting up for him.

"It's a digital video camera with 3-D sound," Sherman said. "It has high-def 1080 resolution with freeze-frame and instant replay. And check out the built-in tape editor, sound mixer, drum machine, projector, DVD player, keyboard, and sandwich maker."

I made a loud gulping sound. I couldn't help it. "Not bad," I muttered. "If that's the best you can do."

"Let me show you how it works," Sherman said. He pushed a lot of buttons, moved a mouse around, clicked a lot of dials—and handed me a ham and Swiss sandwich.

"Pretty good," I said. "But you forgot the mustard."

Sherman studied his machine. "Weird. I *asked* for mustard."

I shook my head. "Nice equipment, Sherman," I said. "But I can make a better movie with my cell phone."

"Good luck, Bernie," he said. "Here come the kids who want to try out for *my* movie."

I turned and saw a long line of kids running toward us. April-May was at the front of the line, followed by ... followed by ...

FEENMAN and CRENCH?!

My best buddies in the whole world? Trying out for Sherman's movie??

"Traitors!"

I shouted. "What's up with you two? What are you *doing* here?"

Crench flashed me a grin. "Yo, Big B," he said. "We heard everyone in Sherman's movie gets free sandwiches!"

Chapter 9

GIANT MONSTER ANTS UP CLOSE

That night, I paced back and forth in my room, thinking, thinking hard. I smelled rubber burning, but I knew it was just the Bernie B. brain, sizzling away.

Did I have any movie ideas?

Not exactly.

Earlier that night, we snuck into Joe Sweety's room and tried to turn him into a mummy. But that ended badly, with me being strangled by Joe for about twenty minutes.

Now I needed a *new* idea. Something a little less painful.

"Yo, Big B!" Belzer called. He came bouncing into my room, carrying about 800 pounds of brown hair in his arms.

"You got a haircut?" I said.

He shook his head. "No. It's a costume—see?" He held it up.

"Is that your Halloween costume?" I asked. "You're going as a smelly pile of hair?"

He shook his head again. "No. It's a gorilla costume. I thought we could use it for a scary movie. You know. Like *King Kong IV* or something."

"Belzer, where'd you get it?" I asked.

"My mother sent it to me," he said. "She thought it was pajamas."

I gagged and held my nose. "Belzer, get it out of here!" I cried. "It...it smells worse than Beast!"

He turned and slumped away, leaving a trail of gross gorilla hair on the floor.

I held my nose for about ten minutes, till the smell started to fade. Then I had an idea.

I hurried downstairs to Billy the Brain's room.

I told you—Billy is the biggest brainiac at Rotten School. I knew he'd have a *million* great movie ideas.

"Yo, Brain, what's up?" I called, stepping into his room.

He was leaning over a big glass case, a camcorder pressed to his face. I stepped up beside him. "What is this?" I asked.

"An ant farm," he said. "I filled it with about a thousand ants."

"Cool," I said. "And you're studying them for Mr. Boring's science class?"

"No," he said. "I'm making a horror video. Check it out. If I use my telescopic lens and go in really close, I can make the ants look like giants!"

"Excellent!" I said. I *told* you the dude is a genius. "What's your movie called?"

"*Giant Monster Ants Up Close*," Billy said. "But I've got one major problem."

"Problem?" I asked.

"Yeah. I can't find any ants in here," Billy said. "It's weird how they all disappeared."

I gazed at the glass case. "It's not *too* weird," I said. "You left the lid off."

Billy stared at the empty case. "Oh, well," he said, "I'll just change the name of the movie. I'll call

it *ESCAPE of the Giant Monster Ants.*"

They don't call him Billy the *Brain* for nothing!

I saw ants crawling all over the floor, swarming over his desk and dresser, onto his bed, under his pillow . . . crawling up the back of his shirt.

I started to itch all over. I had to leave.

I stepped out into the hall—and a huge, snarling creature leaped on me—and sank its hot, wet fangs into my throat.

Chapter 10

ME, THE WEREWOLF

"Beast—get off me," I said. I pried his teeth from my neck.

"Awwww, Bernie," he moaned. "How'd you know it was me? Didn't you think I was a werewolf?"

"Werewolves don't drool that much," I said. "Also, werewolves don't wear a school blazer."

He looked down. "Yeah. Maybe you're right. Maybe I should lose the blazer."

"Beast, why are you out in the hall leaping on people?" I asked.

"You were supposed to act scared," Beast said.

"I'm making a movie. It stars me. It's called *Me, the Werewolf.*"

"Good title," I said.

I was impressed. For once, Beast was acting fairly human. Whenever we went to the movies together, he always ate the seat cushion. But now here he was, making his own movie.

I glanced around. "Hel-lo. Just a minute," I said. "There is no one else here. Who is taping you?"

Beast lowered his furry eyebrows. "Taping me? No one," he said. "I'm making this movie by myself."

"But, Beast," I said. "You need someone with a camera . . . someone to shoot the movie. You can't just run up and down the hall jumping on people and biting their throats!"

"Huh?" he said. "I *can't?*"

Chapter 11

MORNING OF THE ROBOT WORM

I spent the night dreaming up scary movie ideas. Too bad I didn't have time to do any homework.

The next morning, I walked into Mrs. Heinie's class and flashed her a big smile. I knew I'd have to fake it today. Use the good old Bernie B. charm.

"You're looking terrific today, Mrs. H.," I said. "Those bright red earrings you're wearing are totally awesome!"

"I'm not wearing earrings," she said. "I have an ear infection."

"Oh," I said. "Well . . . it looks good on you." I

hurried to my seat between Feenman and Crench in the back of the room. We always sit in the back. Mrs. Heinie is totally nearsighted, and she can't see us back there.

Flora and Fauna, the Peevish twins, sit in front of me. They were flipping frantically through their textbooks.

"We didn't do our homework," Flora whispered. "We were too busy working on our movie."

"What's your movie about?" I asked.

"It's about a virus that, when you get it, you can't stop pinching your sister," she said. "It's way scary." She reached over and pinched her sister's leg as hard as she could.

"YEOOOWWW!"

Fauna screamed. Her leg flew up and kicked the boy in front of her.

"See? Scary!" Flora whispered. "We've both got a lot of purple bruises, but I think we're going to win."

She let out a scream as Fauna pinched her shoulder.

Sherman Oaks turned around with a big grin on his face. "I'm making my movie right now," he whispered. "See that giant robot worm with the dripping fangs against the wall?"

I turned to the front. Yes, there was definitely a giant brown worm with fangs behind Mrs. Heinie.

"It comes from Japan," Sherman said. "I can control it with this little remote unit in my hand. It's a robot covered in real worm skin."

"How do they get the skin off worms?" Feenman asked.

"Don't even think about it," Sherman whispered. "I'm using it for my movie, *Morning of the Robot Worm*. Every time Mrs. Heinie turns her back, the worm will creep up closer to her. Great suspense, huh?"

At the end of the row, Chipmunk jumped up from his seat. He was staring at the giant worm and shaking all over. "T-t-oo s-scary!" he stammered. "We're being attacked. Run for your lives!"

Chipmunk took a running leap and dove out the window. Luckily, our classroom is in the basement. He didn't have far to fall.

Near the front of the room, Billy the Brain had ants crawling in his hair and on the back of his neck. My friend Nosebleed was videoing Billy as he scratched and squirmed.

"OWWWWWW!"

Fauna let out another scream. Her right arm was black and blue from all the pinching.

Near the window, Beast howled up at the sky like a werewolf.

Mrs. Heinie tapped her desk with a ruler to get everyone quiet. "I hope you've all read your homework," she said.

"Yes, we have!" we all lied.

"Can anyone tell me what today's chapter was about?" she asked. "How about you, Wes?"

Wes Updood squirmed in his chair. "Uh . . . it's like jelly in a jar," he said. "No worries, you know. Just jelly in a jar."

Mrs. Heinie squinted at him through her thick glasses. "Are you making any sense at all?" she asked.

"Please, no hints," Wes said. "Let me guess. Is it jelly in a jar?"

"Did you read the chapter?" Mrs. H. asked him.

Wes nodded. "Does jelly jiggle in a jar?"

Mrs. Heinie shook her head. "Wes, I don't think you read the chapter," she said.

Wes blinked a few times. "Can I go to the bathroom?" he asked.

She frowned at him. "Class just started. Why do you want to go to the bathroom?"

"Just trying to think of something to say," Wes replied.

Mrs. Heinie let out a sigh. "I don't think any of you did your homework," she said. "I think you're all working on your scary videos and not doing your schoolwork."

"No, no!"

"Not true!"

"No way!"

we all protested.

And that's when Sherman lost control of the robot worm. And it slid up behind Mrs. Heinie and bit her on the butt!

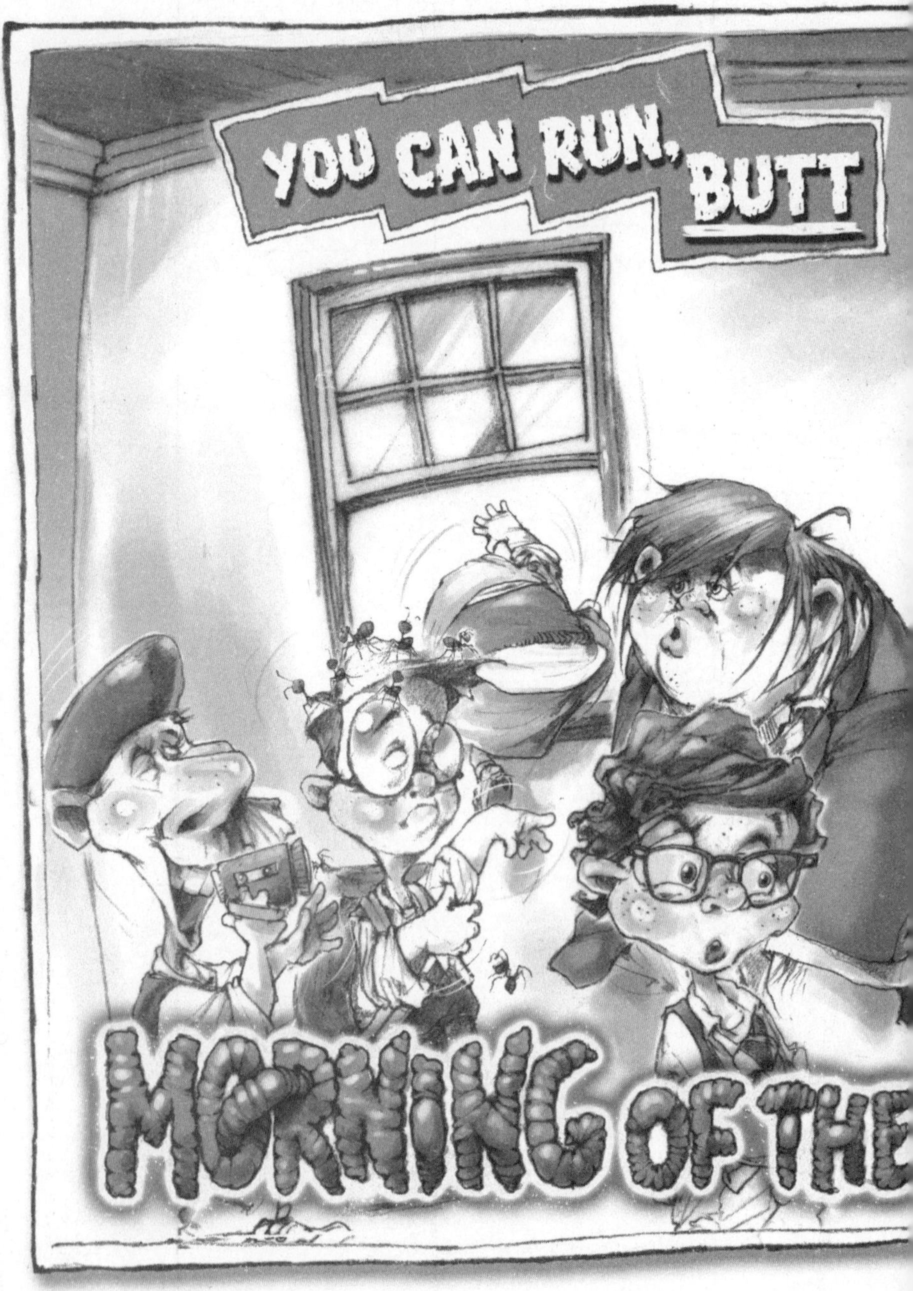
YOU CAN RUN, BUTT
MORNING OF THE

Chapter 12

LOUSY NIGHT AT THE ZOO

"I'm not happy," Mrs. Heinie said, after she finished screaming. "I don't like being attacked by giant snakes in my classroom."

"It's not a giant snake," Sherman said. "It's a giant worm."

"I should punish you all," Mrs. H. said. "I should keep you from going on the overnight on Friday."

Overnight?

With all the movie mania, I'd forgotten all about it.

"But it's too late to cancel it," Mrs. H. said. "I'm sure you all remember that Friday night is the annual sleepover night at the zoo."

Everyone cheered. Sherman made the giant robot worm bob its head up and down as if it was cheering along with us. This sounded like a cool night.

Once a year school groups get to spend the night at the Lousy Town Zoo. I know, I know. It's a funny name. You see, the zoo was named after the man who paid for it, Louie B. Lousy.

Lousy Zoo Night is pretty awesome. We get a night tour of the zoo. They give us a pizza dinner. Then we set up tents and sleep in the gorilla house.

How cool is that?

Sherman turned around and flashed me a thumbs-up. "This is perfect," he said. "I can shoot another movie at the zoo in the dark. I'll call it *Horror Zoo*. Totally creepy. I can't lose!"

Feenman tugged my arm. "Bernie, what are we going to do?" he whispered.

"About what?" I said.

"It's one week to Halloween," Feenman said. "And we haven't even *started* our movie."

"No problem," I told him. "Don't even think about it. We've already won."

"Won? How do we win? We've got nothing!" Feenman said.

"Trust me," I said. "I have the winning idea. No way we can lose."

I tapped Belzer on the head to get his attention. He spun around in his seat. "What's up, Big B?"

"Belzer—get that gorilla costume," I said. "I want you to bring it to the zoo."

"Huh?" His mouth dropped open. "But, Bernie—you said it smells worse than Beast!"

"Belzer, what do you care about a little smell?" I said. "You're gonna be a star!"

Chapter 13

ATTACK OF THE ROOT BEER

Friday night. Lousy Zoo Night. I sat near the front of the school bus and silently sang a little song to myself:

Bernie, you're so smart.
I hope we never part.
I'm your brain, and I can't complain
Because you are so smart.

You like to scheme and plan
Because you are the man!
You'll outsmart Sherman

La–la–la–la–la
What rhymes with Sherman?

I couldn't think of a rhyme, so the song had to end. But I sang it to myself a few times anyway. It brought a smile to my face.

Don't you ever write songs in your head?

Hel-lo. Was I excited?

Does a crocodile have lips?

My heart was pumping. I could hardly sit still as we bounced our way to the zoo. Belzer sat next to me. I kept punching him in the shoulder. "You're the man, Belzer. You're the man!" I kept repeating.

Belzer stared at me and rubbed his shoulder. "Are you okay, Bernie?"

"Awesomely okay!" I replied.

And why shouldn't I be?

I finally had the genius idea that would win the Horror Movie Contest. My scheme would win the contest—*and* ruin Sherman's movie!

No wonder I was writing songs to myself!

The bus rumbled through town. Behind me, Beast shook up two cans of root beer, pulled the tops, and sprayed root beer over the last five rows of kids.

That dude is a riot.

Flora and Fauna Peevish were pinching each other and screaming....

"No, I'm not!"

"Yes, you are!"

"I'm not! I'm not!"

"Yes, you are! I can prove it!"

"Ouch! That hurt!"

"Well, stop pinching me!"

"Then admit you're wrong!"

"*You're* wrong! Liar! Liar!"

I jumped up and walked back to their seat. "Yo. What are you two fighting about?" I asked.

They stared at each other for a long time.

"Uh...I don't remember," Flora said.

"I don't remember, either," Fauna snapped angrily. "Who asked *you*, Bernie Big Mouth?"

"Yeah. Get out of our faces," Flora said. "We were having a nice family talk till you butted in!"

"Okay, okay," I said, backing away. Talk about scary! I could videotape their "family talks" and win the contest!

I looked toward the back of the bus and saw Mrs. Heinie leaning over Chipmunk. Chipmunk had ducked down behind the seat in front of him. I could see he was trying to hide.

"It's too scary," he said to Mrs. H. "I can't sleep with big, hairy gorillas. I just can't."

"But the gorillas are in their cages," Mrs. Heinie told him. "You'll be safe and sound in your own tent."

"Can't I stay on the bus?" Chipmunk asked in a trembling whisper. "I'll just sleep here. Okay?"

"No one sleeps on the bus," Mrs. H. insisted.

Beast had an evil grin on his face. He shook up another can of root beer and sent a frothy spray splashing over Chipmunk.

"Mrs. Heinie, can't you make him *stop*?" Chipmunk whined.

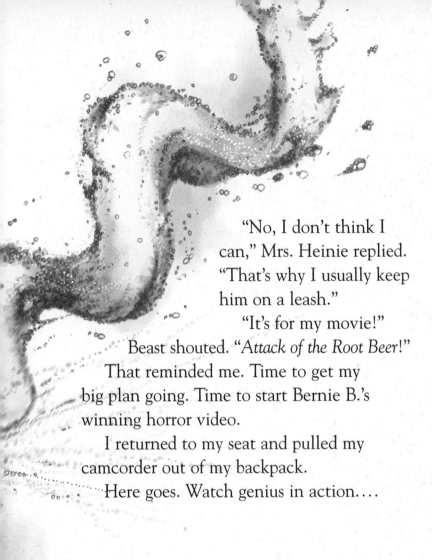

"No, I don't think I can," Mrs. Heinie replied. "That's why I usually keep him on a leash."

"It's for my movie!" Beast shouted. "*Attack of the Root Beer!*" That reminded me. Time to get my big plan going. Time to start Bernie B.'s winning horror video.

I returned to my seat and pulled my camcorder out of my backpack.

Here goes. Watch genius in action....

Chapter 14

THE MAKING OF HORROR ZOO

I walked back to Sherman's seat, raised the camcorder, and started to tape him.

"Hey, what's up with this?" Sherman asked. "What do you think you're doing?"

"Just act natural," I said. "Pretend I'm not here."

"Excuse me?" Sherman said, hiding his face from my camera. "What's the big idea, Bernie?"

"Ignore me," I said. "Just act normal."

"But—but—" he sputtered.

"What's the name of your horror movie again?" I asked him.

"*Horror Zoo*," he answered.

"Well, I'm doing a documentary," I said. "It's called *The Making of* Horror Zoo."

Sherman lowered his hands from his face and stared at me. "You mean you're making a documentary about *me?*"

I nodded. "Yeah. It's a behind-the-scenes thing. Starring you."

He thought about it. A smile spread over his face. "Sweet!" he said finally. "I guess you finally realized who the master moviemaker is around here."

"You got it," I said. I moved the camcorder right into his nose for a close-up. "Wiggle your nostrils," I said. "Good. That's good. Very scary."

He pushed the lens out of his nose. "So you're just gonna follow me and my crew around and tape everything we do?"

"You got it," I said again.

Only he *didn't* get it.

I didn't tell him the whole truth. My film was *not* about the making of Sherman's film. It was actually about how Sherman and his pals try to make a movie—but get *scared to DEATH!*

Chapter 15

SCREAM, SHERMAN, SCREAM!

My buddies and I had it all worked out. Our plan was to *terrify* Sherman and Wes and their pals. And get it all on tape for *my* movie—*Scream, Sherman, Scream!*

How could I lose?

The bus pulled up to the zoo's front gate. It was decorated with jack-o'-lanterns, giant spiders, and lots of cobwebs. As we drove through, I saw that the whole zoo was decorated for Halloween. Mummies, scarecrows, and coffins poked out from trees and bushes. Strange orange lights cut through swirling, thick fog.

Perfect.

I heard creepy organ music. And the sound of wolves howling in the distance.

Even more perfect.

"I'll just stay here," Chipmunk was telling Mrs. Heinie. "Someone should guard the bus—right?"

But she pulled him out with the rest of us.

We carried our bags and tents to the gorilla house. It was a cold, cloudy night. No moon in the sky. The wind rustled the trees and blew dead leaves over our feet.

Totally scary.

The big gorillas stared at us through their cage bars. One of them moved his finger over his lips and went, "Buh-buh-buh."

What did *that* mean?

"People. People! Gather around!" A tall, chubby man in a green uniform and green cap waved us over to him. "I'm your guide for the night," he said.

He held up a silver badge. "I'm a zoo ranger. I guess my parents *really* wanted me to work in a zoo. They named me Sandy, and my last name is Eggozoo."

He waved for us to follow him. He guided us along a narrow path that led past several low buildings. Creepy music poured from hidden speakers. Jack-o'-lanterns grinned at us.

Sandy Eggozoo opened a door and held it for us to go inside. "This is the snake house," he said. "As you can see, our snakes are all behind glass, so you can view them easily."

I stared into a glass cage. A huge, blue snake, curled around a log, stared back at me with its beady, black eyes.

"The snakes move a lot at night," Sandy said. "You guys are lucky. The python was fed this afternoon. We feed it mice. You can still see the mouse bulging in its throat."

"Ooh, gross," April-May June said.

Beast licked his lips. "Do you have any mice left over?" he asked.

"We'll eat later," Mrs. Heinie told him. "We're going to have pizza."

"Pizza is good, too," Beast said.

The only snake I was interested in was Sherman Oaks. He and his pals walked over to the python cage and started to set up their movie equipment.

They turned a spotlight on April-May. She was the star of Sherman's movie. Behind her, the python raised its head and slid toward the glass. Sherman set up his camera.

"Lights, camera, action," I whispered to Feenman and Crench. That was our signal to get to work. Time to start terrifying Sherman and everyone working on his movie.

We started over to him. But Billy the Brain stepped in front of us.

"Yo. Dudes. Here's something I bet you didn't know," Billy said. "If you cut off a snake's head, it'll grow a new one in a few days."

"Very cool," I said. "You know everything, Brain. But we're kinda in a hurry and—"

"Here's another interesting fact," Billy said. "The snake is the only animal that doesn't brush its teeth."

"Is that true?" Feenman said, scratching his head. "Wow. That's amazing."

"Tell us some more," Crench said.

I gave Crench a push. "Did you forget we've got things to do?"

I pulled Feenman and Crench away from Billy. We slipped over to where Sherman and his gang were starting to videotape their movie scene.

I handed the camcorder to Feenman. "Just push the red button to record," I whispered.

Then I turned to Crench. "Have you got it?"

He nodded. And pulled a big, black rubber snake out from under his jacket. The snake had two long, pointy fangs. It bobbed up and down in Crench's hand. Its eyes glowed yellow.

It looked real and alive.

"Feenman, start recording when Crench tosses the snake," I whispered.

I turned to Crench. "Wait till April-May starts reading her lines. Then toss the snake right in front of her. Ready, dudes?"

I hated to do this to my girlfriend. But this was going to be a great opening scene for our movie, *Scream, Sherman, Scream!*

We crept a little closer. In its cage, the python seemed to be watching us.

"Okay. Action!" I whispered.

Feenman raised the camcorder to his face.

Crench tossed the big snake.

"Poison Mamba!" I screamed at the top of my lungs.

"POISON MAMBA! IT ESCAPED!"

Chapter 16

SNAKES ON MY LEG

A perfect toss! The rubber snake bounced on the floor and curled around April-May's leg.

She shot her hands into the air and let out a shrill scream of horror. Sherman screamed, too. He tripped and stumbled to the floor with a loud *thud*.

Awesome.

Life was sweet.

I turned to Feenman. "Did you get that on tape?"

He nodded. "Hope I didn't shake the camcorder too much. I was laughing pretty hard."

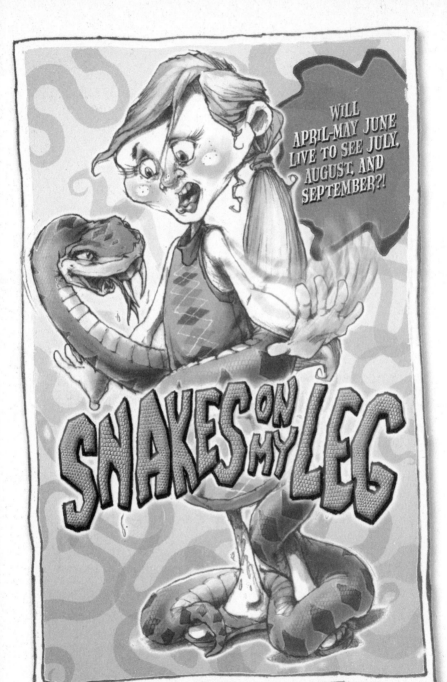

"We totally messed them up," Crench said. We slapped knuckles.

Sherman climbed to his feet and came stomping over to us, swinging his fists.

Uh-oh. The dude looked angry.

"Sherman, it was an accident—" I started.

But he grabbed my hand and shook it. "Thanks, Bernie," he said. "That was brilliant!"

My mouth dropped open. "Brilliant?"

"I couldn't get April-May to scream," Sherman said. "But you did it for me."

He slapped me a low five. "Thanks, pal. You're a real help. Now we can go on to the next big scene. Know what? You've given me a *great* idea. I'm going to call my movie *Snakes on My Leg*."

He flashed me a thumbs-up. "Thanks for all the help!"

Chapter 17

MOVIE IN MY HEAD

Our next chance came in the Tunnel of Darkness.

"This building is for our nocturnal animals," Sandy Eggozoo said. "Creatures who only come out at night."

It was pitch-black in this building, except for a dim, red light.

"Watch out for the bats," Mrs. Heinie called. "I can see their shadows on the ceiling."

"First you walk through the Tunnel of Darkness," Sandy said. "The bat cave is at the other end. Take your time going through the tunnel. You'll see lots of interesting creatures."

I grabbed Feenman and Crench. "We're not gonna take our time," I whispered. "Let's move. We need to get to the other end of the tunnel."

We pushed past kids gaping at a skinny tree sloth. Some other dudes stood in front of a glass case, pointing at a funny-looking animal that had a furry body and a face that looked kinda like a bat's. It was called a slow loris.

We had to get to the end of the tunnel first to set up our next trick. But there was Billy the Brain again. He blocked our path, eager to show us how much he knew.

"Dudes, you know the funny thing about bats?" he asked.

"Billy, we're in a hurry," I said. "Maybe—"

"The word *BATS* is spelled the same forward and backward. Isn't that amazing?"

"Wow. I never thought about that!" Crench said.

"Cool," Feenman agreed.

Sometimes I think all my friends are morons.

"The slow loris isn't really slow," Billy said. "It's just that every other animal in the world is faster. So that makes the loris *look* slow."

"Billy, you know *everything*!" Feenman said.

"Are you working on a scary movie?" Crench asked him.

Billy nodded. "It's called *Movie in My Head*, and it takes place entirely in my head."

"Awesome," Crench said. "Can't wait to see it."

"You *can't* see it," Billy replied. "It's only in my head!"

I pulled my two buddies away. "Catch you later, Brain!" I called.

"Let me know if you need to know anything," Billy called back.

Kids were moving through the tunnel, nearing the end. My buddies and I had to work fast if we were going to give Sherman and his pals a real scare.

"Have you got it?" I asked Crench. "Quick." I stuck out my hand.

He pulled the can out from under his jacket. A can of spray-on cobwebs. Feenman pulled out a can, too.

We both started spraying a thick blanket of cobwebs over the tunnel exit. The stuff was wet and sticky and creepy.

"This is gonna be sweet!" I said. "When Sherman and his friends walk into the webs, they'll totally freak. They'll be scratching and screaming and trying to pull the webs off their faces."

I slid the camcorder into Feenman's hand. "Get ready. Don't miss this. Here they come."

Squinting into the deep, red light, we waited for our classmates to come to the exit. Some dudes were still gawking at the weird animals in their glass cages.

Sherman was busy taping April-May as she pretended to be attacked by a slow loris.

Slowly they made their way toward the exit.

"Get ready. Here they come," I whispered to Feenman. "Wait for it. . . . Wait for it. . . . This isn't going to be pretty!"

April-May stepped into the tunnel exit. Sherman and Wes followed.

"SPIDERS!"

I screamed. "LOOK OUT! SPIDERS!"

I held my breath, waiting for them to scream and

start pulling at the sticky webs.

But they walked right through and kept walking.

Mrs. Heinie walked through, followed by several other kids.

"What's up with THIS?" I cried.

I pulled out a flashlight and shined it at the exit. "Beast!" I exclaimed. "What are you doing here?"

I didn't have to wait for his answer.

I saw.

Beast had slurped up all the cobwebs. He had sticky stuff all over his grinning face.

He let out a two-minute burp. "I love this stuff," he said. "It's my favorite vegetable!"

Chapter 18

ESCAPE OF THE MAD, MAD, MAD GORILLA

Okay, okay. That didn't work, either.

No problem.

Does Bernie B. know how to quit?

I don't know the meaning of the word *quit*.

I'd been saving the best for last. I had a plan to get *everyone* screaming.

It would make my new horror video—*Escape of the Mad, Mad, Mad Gorilla*—the scariest movie of all. Soon B. A. Gool would be *begging* me to come help him with his new film.

Sandy Eggozoo finished our tour. We had our

pizza dinner. Then it was time to settle down for the night.

Our tents were lined up in two rows down the middle of the gorilla house. On both sides, gorillas paced their cages, scratching their heads, watching us.

They made low gorilla grunts to one another. As if they were asking, "Why are these freaks sleeping in our house?"

I knew some of the gorillas must be asking, "Who is that totally cool dude named Bernie Bridges?"

Mrs. Heinie and Sandy Eggozoo made sure our sleeping bags were ready and that we were all in place. We were sleeping four kids to a tent.

Except for me. I had a letter from the nurse saying that I'm allergic to other kids. So I had a tent of my own.

Which I needed, because I had to store Belzer's gorilla costume. It smelled more disgusting than the *real* gorillas. But I didn't care.

It was going to help me film the greatest scene in the history of horror movies.

I peeked out of my tent. The lights in the gorilla house had been turned down low. The gorillas grunted and groaned and shuffled around in their cages.

I hoped they enjoyed the excitement, too. It was probably a little boring being a gorilla.

Some kids were still talking and giggling in their tents. I waited till it grew quiet and most kids were asleep.

Then I lifted the flap of the tent beside mine. "Belzer, wake up!" I called in a hoarse whisper. "It's showtime!"

Belzer staggered out of the tent, yawning and rubbing his eyes. He had his pajamas on backward. Why? I didn't want to go there.

Feenman poked his head out of the tent. "Ready when you are, Bernie," he whispered. He raised the camcorder.

I waved Feenman back into the tent. "Wait till I get Belzer into his costume," I whispered.

Belzer let out a loud yawn.

"Shhhh!" I clapped a hand over his mouth. "Don't wake everyone up. You'll ruin the surprise."

I pulled him into my tent and shoved the gorilla costume into his hands. "Hurry. Get into it."

He gagged. "But, Bernie—it STINKS!"

"What makes you think *you* smell any better?" I replied. "Stop stalling, Belzer. You want to go to Hollywood—don't you? You want to be a star? Get dressed."

I leaped out of the tent. That hairy costume really did *reek*!

A few minutes later, Belzer stepped out. He looked so real, a few of the gorillas started jumping up and down in their cages.

"Go, Belzer!" I exclaimed. "King Kong Jr.! You're the MAN! I mean, gorilla!" I slapped the big guy a high five.

"I . . . I can't SEE!" Belzer whined from inside the gorilla head. Bernie, I can't see out of this thing!"

"Don't worry about it," I said. I gave him a little push. "Go out there and be a STAR!"

I whispered to Feenman in the tent. "Time to go to work. Get the camcorder ready. We're gonna make an award-winner!"

The plan was simple.

I flash on all the lights in the gorilla house.

I shout at the top of my lungs: "WILD GORILLA ESCAPED! WILD GORILLA ESCAPED!"

Belzer the Gorilla starts roaring and running through the tents and sleeping bags, waving his furry arms.

Kids jump out of their tents. Jump out of their *skin*! Crying. Running for their lives. We get Sherman screaming his head off.

A true horror story. An *awesome* scene of total panic.

And Feenman gets it all on tape.

Bye-bye, Sherman. Take a walk, dude. No way you can compete with a MAD, MAD, MAD GORILLA!

B. A. Gool will say, "Bernie, how did you make it look so REAL? I need you to be my *partner*!"

And I'll say, "My buddies have to come to Hollywood, too." Because even when I'm a *huge* star, I won't forget the friends who helped get me there.

Okay. Here goes.

I crept over to the light switches—and clicked them all on....

Chapter 19

ATTACK OF THE KLUTZ!

Belzer let out a roar. He ran about three feet and stumbled over a tent.

The tent crashed to the floor under him, and two kids crawled out, looking totally dazed.

"WILD GORILLA!"

I screamed.

"WILD GORILLA ESCAPED!"

Belzer picked himself up and went roaring through the rows of tents.

"WILD GORILLA!" I shouted.

Feenman raised the camcorder to his eye and started to shoot.

I stood against a wall, my heart pounding, and waited for the scene of total panic to start.

Kids began popping out of their tents. I heard a few startled screams.

Yes. Yes! It was happening!

Belzer the Gorilla stumbled again. He bounced off a tent and kept running, roaring and waving his arms above his head.

More kids climbed to their feet. Yes. *Yes!*

But, whoa. Wait.

I saw Wes Updood raise a camcorder to his face and point it at Belzer. Two more kids pulled cameras out. On the other side of the room, I saw April-May, Flora and Fauna Peevish, and Jennifer Ecch—all with cameras raised.

Belzer's gorilla head tilted and almost fell off. He let out a roar.

I saw more kids reaching for camcorders. Some

were recording the scene on cell phones.

Sherman Oaks had his fancy camera trained on Belzer.

"No. Please—no! Not Sherman! Not Sherman, too!" I wailed.

I slumped against the wall. I let out a long sigh.

My plan…my beautiful plan…

Where was the panic? Where was the scene of total *horror?*

No screaming. No running.

Everyone was making MY MOVIE!

Belzer the Gorilla stumbled again. The poor guy couldn't see a thing in that costume.

Dozens of camcorders followed his every move.

Belzer staggered forward, waving his arms, struggling to catch his balance.

CLANNNNNG!

He fell face-forward against a gorilla cage. Inside the cage, the gorilla reached out—and tapped Belzer on the head!

"YIIIIIKES!" Belzer let out a shriek. He tore off his gorilla head and heaved it against a wall. Then he took off running—out the door!

Kids were laughing now. Laughing and slapping high fives and touching knuckles.

Feenman lowered his camcorder. "Bernie," he said, "it's a total *disaster*!"

I shrugged. "Maybe B. A. Gool would like a *comedy* called *Attack of the Klutz*!"

Chapter 20

SCREAM, FEENMAN AND CRENCH, SCREAM!

Halloween night. Party night. B. A. Gool night!

Two grinning skeletons greeted everyone at the Student Center as we entered the party. The skeletons were made of papier-mâché and shook and rattled in the cold wind.

A shivering mummy held the door open for everyone. I recognized Mr. Pocketlint, one of the dorm parents, inside the bandages.

Orange and black streamers were stretched across the ceiling. Paper bats flapped low over our heads. Casper the Friendly Ghost was pasted on one wall.

"Party time!" I said, slapping Feenman on the shoulder.

It was a costume party. Feenman was dressed as Crench, and Crench was dressed as Feenman.

I saw Belzer in his gorilla suit. Actually, I *smelled* him first—then I saw him!

I painted a lightning bolt on my forehead and

SCREAM, FEENMAN &

Go Feenman!
Go Crench! Go Ape!

came as Harry Potter. That's because I'm a *wizard* at moviemaking.

I did a great editing job on the tape Feenman had shot. I mixed together close-up shots of the real gorillas with shots of Belzer staggering around. Then, in the dorm, I had Feenman and Crench scream and pretend to be frightened.

My video was called *Scream, Feenman and Crench, Scream!*, and it was terrifying. I knew I couldn't lose.

I gazed around the crowded party. A lot of kids

were dressed as monsters and vampires. I guess they were trying to impress B. A. Gool.

I saw a really hairy, frightening werewolf gulping down a slice of pizza. No. It wasn't a werewolf. It was Beast without a costume.

I saw Chipmunk hiding behind the punch bowl. He was shaking and shivering. Poor guy. Halloween is a scary time for him. I knew Chipmunk would be glad when this whole Horror Movie Contest was over.

Where was B. A. Gool?

I was dying for him to announce my video as the winner.

Sherman Oaks came over to me. He wore a green mummy costume.

"Sherman, dude—a *green* mummy?" I said. "Why is it green? Because it's totally moldy?"

He grinned his sixty-five-tooth grin. "No way. It's green cuz it's made out of five-dollar bills." He shook his head. "I feel so sorry for kids in fourth grade who aren't millionaires yet."

"Don't feel bad," I said. I patted his shoulder. Actually, I tried to pull off a few fives. But they were glued on tight.

"I feel sorry for dudes in fourth grade who *aren't* going to win B. A. Gool's contest," I said. "Do you want to congratulate me now, Sherman? Or do you want to stand in line later?"

And at that moment, B. A. Gool stepped onto the stage. "Happy Halloween, boys and ghouls!" he shouted. "I've come to announce the winner of the Horror Movie Contest."

Chapter 21

I'M SCARED!

"And the winner is ..." B. A. Gool said. And then he stopped.

"Why don't I *show* you the winning video first?" he said.

He pulled down a movie screen from the ceiling. "Okay, roll it," he said. And a few seconds later the winning video started.

A face came on the screen.

I squinted at it. What's up with *that*? It wasn't a face from *my* video!

"Is that Chipmunk?" I whispered to Feenman.

"Why is he trembling and shaking and quaking like that?"

Feenman shrugged. "Beats me."

You couldn't see what he was afraid of. You could

I'M SCARED

THE MOVIE YOU'VE ALL BEEN WAITING FOR — STARRING CHIPMUNK LOOKING TOTALLY TERRIFIED!

only see his face. You could see that he was totally terrified.

"This is the most original video I've ever seen," Gool boomed. "You can *feel* this boy's terror. What amazing acting! You really believe that he is scared to death. And he taped it all by himself!"

I let out a long moan. Is this really *happening*? *Chipmunk* made the scariest movie?

Gool turned to Chipmunk. "What is your video called, young man?"

Chipmunk trembled for a few seconds. Then he finally answered in a tiny voice, "It's called *I'm Scared*."

"Brilliant!" Gool cried, pumping his fists into the air. "Brilliant job! You win! Chipmunk, you get to play the victim in my next film!"

"Really?" Chipmunk said. "I get to play a *victim*?

YEAAAAAAA!"

Chipmunk let out a cheer, and so did everyone else.

"YEAAAAAA!"

My mouth had dropped to my knees. I tried to push it closed, but it wouldn't go.

I stood there frozen, unable to move.

Chipmunk is the winner? How could he win?

He didn't even have a gorilla suit!

Finally I got my legs working again. I hurried across the room to Chipmunk. I slapped him a high five, we touched knuckles, and did the secret Rotten House Handshake.

I put a hand on his shoulder. "Congratulations, Chipper," I said. "I'm sure you'll want me to come to Hollywood with you to help you out in your scenes. I'll go pack my bags."

He brushed my hand away. "Please," he said, "don't touch a star."

He stuck his nose into the air. "Sorry, Bernie—no autographs today. I'm just not in the mood. Please back away. You're crowding me. Give a star room to breathe."

"But—but—but—" I sputtered.

"Sorry," he said, pushing me aside. "My limo is waiting outside. Wish I could give you a lift. But I never let lowly fans travel with me. Ta-ta."

He gave a little wave, then hurried out the door.

I turned to Sherman. "Now, *that's* SCARY!" I said.

HERE'S A SNEAK PEEK AT BOOK #15

R.L. STINE'S

ROTTEN SCHOOL

NUMERO UNO

"Uno!" I cried. I slapped my cards down on the table. "Pay up, guys. Pay up."

Sherman Oaks, that spoiled, rich kid, pulled some bills from his gold money clip. He shook his head. "You've been winning all night, Bernie. I'm down to my last five hundred dollars!"

"When you're hot, you're hot," I said, taking his money."

"Feenman, I *know* you're hiding them," I said.

"Bernie, you're so lucky," Crench groaned. "How can one person win twenty Uno games in a row?"

"It's not luck. It's skill," I said, taking his money. Crench always pays in pennies, but I don't care. I like any coins that jingle.

I reached up to my shoulder and pet Lippy, my adorable parrot.

"*Awwwk. Beak me!*" he squawked. "*BEAK me! I'll pluck your eyes!*"

Who taught him to say those cute things?

He dug his claws into my shoulder as I tickled his feathers.

"*I'll pluck your face!*" he squawked. "*Bite my beak!*" Something warm and gooey plopped onto my shirt.

Across the card table, Sherman's pal Wes Updood was still counting his cards. "Check it out. Gummi worms aren't real worms," he muttered. "They're made out of gummi. Does that mean *real* worms all come from Ohio? I don't *think* so."

Wes is the coolest dude at Rotten School. He's so totally cool, no one can understand a word he says!

He opened his little bottle of vanilla extract and rubbed some on his face. He says it makes a great aftershave lotion.

Wes is in fourth grade—like the rest of us—and of course he doesn't shave. But he's so *way* cool, he uses aftershave anyway.

Feenman yawned so hard he fell off his chair. He rubbed his red eyes. "Bernie, what time is it?"

Sherman raised his *huge* gold watch. The watch has so many jewels and so many functions, it weighs nearly forty pounds. Sherman usually pays a first grader to carry it around for him.

"Whoa," he said, squinting at the flashing dial. "You wouldn't *believe* the temperature on Mars!"

"I just want to know the time," Feenman said.

Sherman stared at his watch. "I . . . I can't find it," he said. "Too many other functions. Want to know the humidity in Caracas, Venezuela?"

"It's six in the morning," I said. I pointed to the clock on the wall.

"Time to pluck your nose!" Lippy chirped.

So cute. I tickled the back of his neck.

"I'll peck your face off!"

"We've been playing all night," Crench groaned. "And Bernie won every game."

I cracked my knuckles. "It's all in the fingers."

Wes Updood handed me some money. "Gotta go chase myself," he said. "You ever chase yourself? It's fun—until you get caught."

He's the coolest dude.

Wes and Sherman stood up, shaking their heads, watching me count my winnings.

"Rather *be* you than *see* you," Wes said as they left.

Did *that* make any sense?

We have our all-night Uno tournaments in a tiny back room in the Student Center. All the lights are out in the building. No one knows we are here. We have to be very careful. I don't know why. But for some reason, Headmaster Upchuck doesn't approve of all-night card games.

Crench jumped to his feet. "Way to go, Big B!" he cried. "You are definitely Numero Uno!" He slapped me a hard high five.

And knocked Lippy off my shoulder.

"*Awwwwwwwk!*" The bird let out a cry as he hit the floor.

"Oh no!" I gasped.

I picked the parrot up in my hands. "Lippy, speak to me!" I cried. "Speak to me!"

LUCKY LIPPY

"*Eat feathers and DIE!*" Lippy squawked.

I let out a long sigh and gently smoothed the cute bird's feathers. "Thank goodness you're okay."

"*Awwwwk. Make my day! Choke on a cuttle-bone!*"

I picked Lippy up and cradled him against my chest.

Feenman squinted at me. "Bernie, why do you bring that squawking bird to all our card games?" he asked.

"Yeah, he's just a stupid bird. What's the big deal?" Crench said.

My two best buddies in the world, and they didn't understand.

"Hel-lo!" I said. "Just a stupid bird? I don't think so! He's a lucky bird."

They both stared at Lippy.

I felt something warm and sticky plop into my hand. "Lippy is a good-luck charm," I explained, wiping my hand off on Crench's jeans. "I can't win without him."

Feenman blinked. "You're joking, right?"

"No joke," I said, tickling Lippy's back. "Haven't you dudes noticed? Every time I bring Lippy to a game, I win big-time."

Feenman and Crench laughed. "Yeah. That bird really knows his cards!" Feenman said. "Maybe we should let him deal!"

"Go ahead and make fun," I said. "But this parrot is totally lucky. And not just for card games. Every time he's with me, he brings me good luck."

"*Awwwwwk.*" Lippy squawked and dropped a huge glob of green bird plop on the floor.

"How lucky is that?" Crench said. "That parrot is totally gross."

"Oh, yeah?" I said. "You guys think you're so smart? Look what Lippy was trying to show me."

I pointed to the floor. Next to the bird plop was a dollar bill.

I picked it up and shoved it into my pocket. "See?" I said. "Someone dropped that money. And why did I find it? Because of Lucky Lippy!"

That made them both stop laughing. They stared at Lippy.

"No joke? That loudmouth pile of feathers is lucky?" Feenman said. "Hey—let me touch him. I want some luck to rub off on me!"

"Yo! Me, too!" Crench cried.

They both pounced on Lippy. Feenman grabbed him around the neck. Crench grabbed him by his claws.

"Let go!" Crench shouted.

"You let go!" Feenman shouted back.

It was an ugly tug-of-war. Feathers flew everywhere. They stretched Lippy out till he was about six feet long!

"Let go of him!" I cried.

8

"*Awwwwwk!*" the parrot squawked. "*I'll peck you till you tweet!*"

I grabbed my adorable pet back and hugged him to my chest. "Stop it!" I screamed. "Are you both nuts? Look what you did to him!"

ABOUT THE AUTHOR

R.L. Stine graduated from Rotten School with a solid D+ average, which put him at the top of his class. He says that his favorite activities at school were Scratching Body Parts and Making Armpit Noises.

In sixth grade, R.L. won the school Athletic Award for his performance in the Wedgie Championships. Unfortunately, after the tournament, his underpants had to be surgically removed.

After graduation, R.L. became well known for writing scary book series such as The Nightmare Room, Fear Street, Goosebumps, and Mostly Ghostly, and a short story collection called Beware!

Today, R.L. lives in New York City, where he is busy writing stories about his school days.

For more information about R.L. Stine, go to www.rottenschool.com and www.rlstine.com